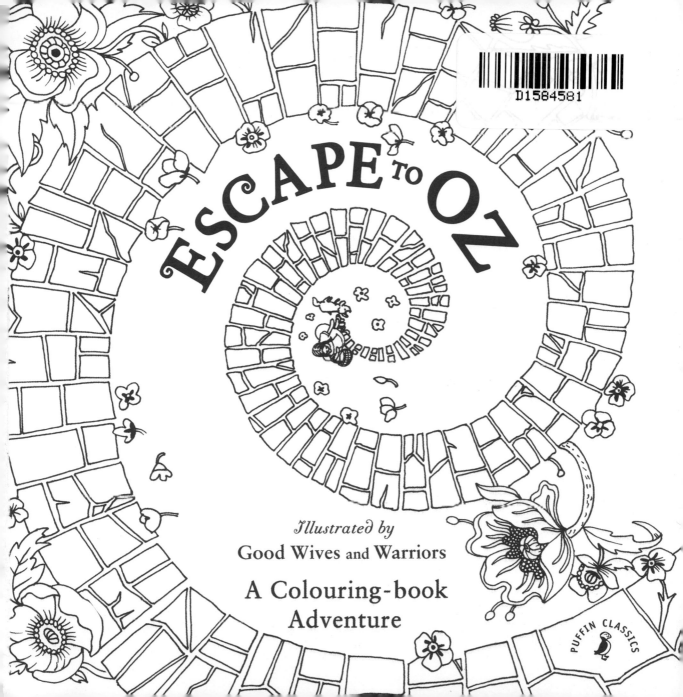

ESCAPE TO OZ

Illustrated by
Good Wives and Warriors

A Colouring-book Adventure

PUFFIN CLASSICS

PUFFIN BOOKS

UK | USA | Canada | Ireland | Australia | India | New Zealand | South Africa

Puffin Books is part of the Penguin Random House group of companies
whose addresses can be found at global.penguinrandomhouse.com.

puffinbooks.com

First published 2016
Illustrations copyright © Good Wives and Warriors, 2016

006

Set in Sabon MT and Bodoni Classic Chancery
Printed in China
A CIP catalogue record for this book is available from the British Library

ISBN: 978-0-141-37548-9

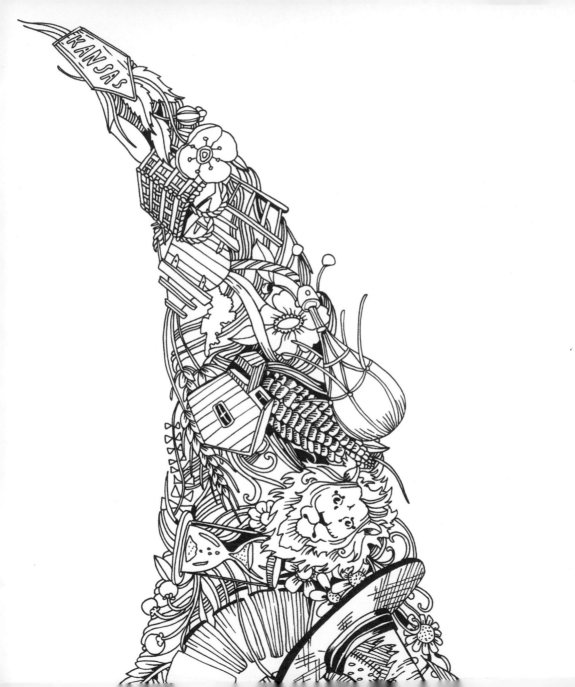

'There's a cyclone coming, Em . . .'

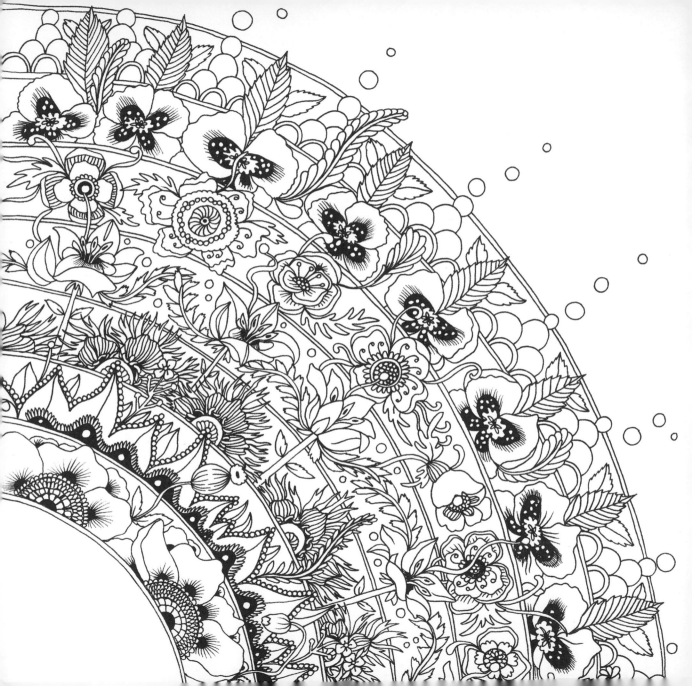

The cyclone had set the house down, very gently – for a cyclone – in the midst of a country of *marvellous beauty* . . .

'You are welcome, most noble Sorceress, to the land of the *Munchkins* . . .'

...just under the corner of the great beam the house rested on, two feet were sticking out, shod in silver shoes with pointed toes.

Toto was a *little black dog*, with long silky hair and small black eyes that twinkled merrily.

'I don't know anything. You see, I am stuffed, so I have no brains at all.'

They started along the path of yellow brick for the *Emerald City.*

EMERALD CITY

One of the big trees had been partly chopped through, and standing beside it, with an uplifted axe in his hands, was a *man made entirely of tin*.

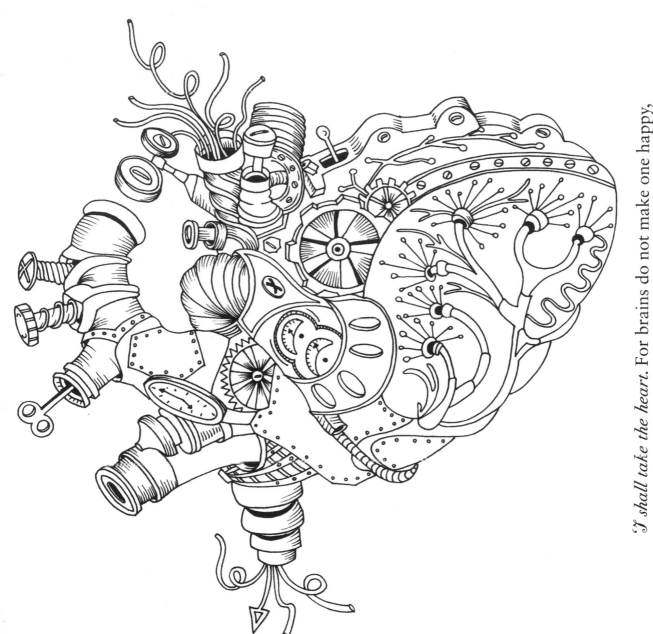

'I shall take the heart. For brains do not make one happy, and happiness is the best thing in the world.'

'The road to the *City of Emeralds* is paved with *yellow brick*,' said the Witch, 'so you cannot miss it.'

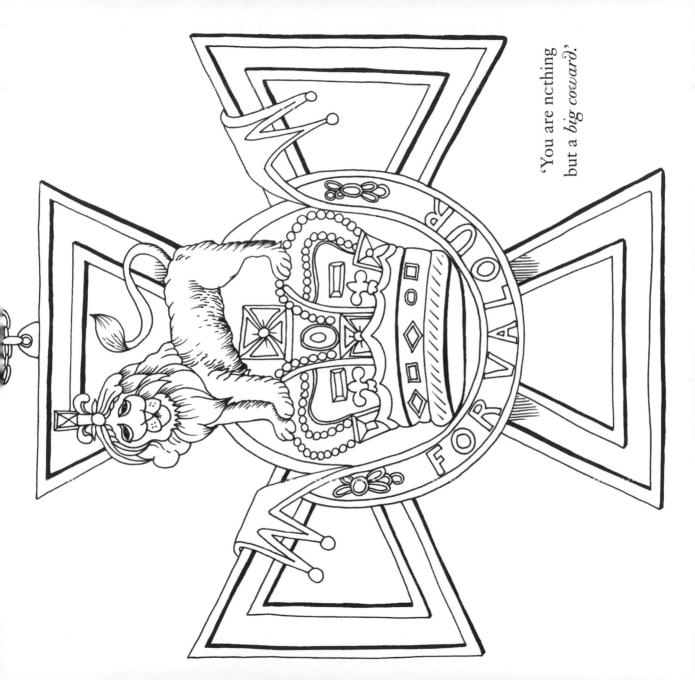

'You are nothing
but a *big coward*.'

Dorothy dreamed of the Emerald City, and of the good Wizard Oz, who would soon send her back to her own home again.

'They are the *Kalidahs*!' said the Cowardly Lion, beginning to tremble.

The stork with her *great claws* grabbed the Scarecrow by the arm.

Her eyes closed in spite of herself and she forgot where she was and fell among the *poppies*, fast asleep.

'Why, I am a Queen – the Queen of all the *field* mice!'

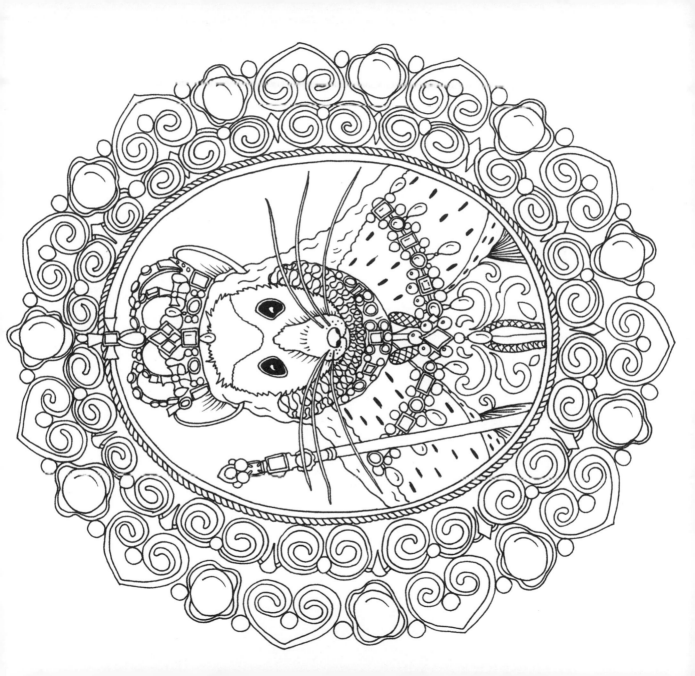

They came from
all directions and there
were thousands of them:
big mice and little mice and
middle-sized mice.

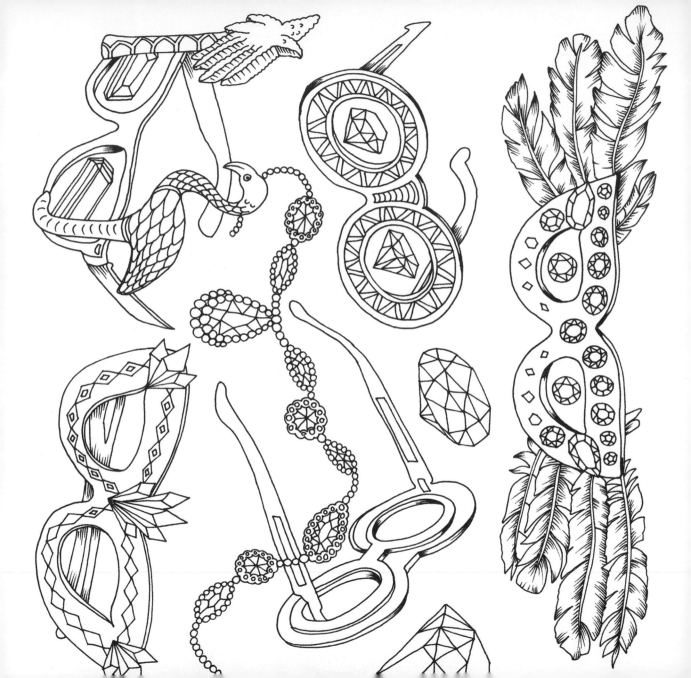

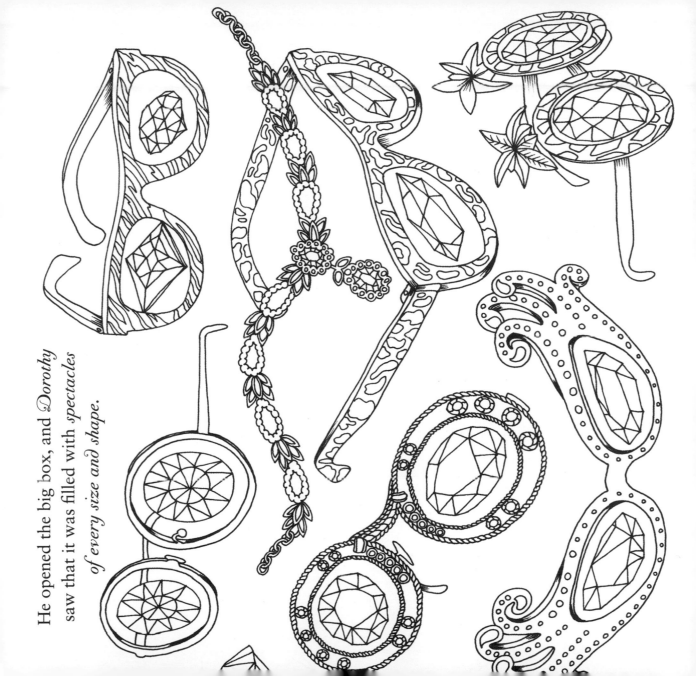

He opened the big box, and *Dorothy* saw that it was filled with *spectacles of every size and shape.*

Even with eyes protected by the green spectacles, Dorothy and her friends were at first dazzled by the brilliancy of the wonderful City.

'But who the real Oz is, when he is in his own form, no living person can tell.'

The *Wicked Witch of the West* had but one eye, yet that was as powerful as a *telescope*.

The little girl was quite frightened when she saw the great pile of *shaggy wolves.*

A great flock of *wild* *crows* came flying towards her, enough to *darken the sky.*

Forthwith there was heard a
great *buzzing in the air* . . .

The sun came out of the dark sky to show the *Wicked Witch* surrounded by a crow

f *monkeys*, each with a pair of *immense* and *powerful wings* on his shoulders.

The *Witch* fell down in a brown, melted, shapeless

mass and began to spread over the kitchen floor.

'I am Oz, the Great and Terrible. Who are you, and why do you seek me?'

Oz, left to himself, smiled to think of his success in giving

the Scarecrow and the *Tin Woodman* and the *Lion* exactly what they thought they wanted.

Coward

Gradually the balloon swelled out and rose into the air,

until finally the basket just touched the ground.

They began walking through *the country of the china people.*

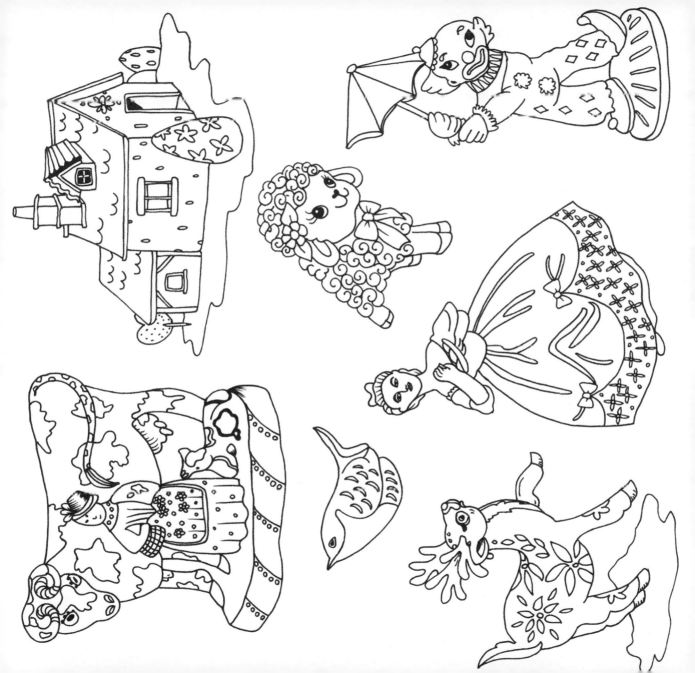

'*True courage* is in facing danger when you are afraid, and that kind of courage you have in plenty.'

It is a most
tremendous
monster, like
a great spider,
with a body as
big as an elephant
and legs as long
as a tree trunk.

Oh, Aunt Em! I'm so glad to be at home again!'